# Anne's
## KINDRED SPIRITS

*To my kindred spirits, near and far* —K.G.

*For Gemma* —A.H.

*With undying gratitude to L.M. Montgomery for creating the classic story on which this book is based.*

Tundra Books, an imprint of Penguin Random House Canada Young Readers, a Penguin Random House Company

Library and Archives Canada Cataloguing in Publication

George, K. (Kallie), 1983-, author

 Anne's kindred spirits / Kallie George ; [illustrated by] Abigail Halpin.

(An Anne chapter book ; 2)

Issued in print and electronic formats.

ISBN 978-1-77049-932-4 (hardcover).—ISBN 978-1-77049-933-1 (EPUB)

 I. Halpin, Abigail, illustrator II. Title.

PS8563.E6257A85 2019      jC813'.6      C2018-906041-7

C2018-906042-5

Published simultaneously in the United States of America by Tundra Books of Northern New York, an imprint of Penguin Random House Canada Young Readers, a Penguin Random House Company

Library of Congress Control Number: 2018962296

Edited by Tara Walker and Jessica Burgess

Designed by Jennifer Griffiths

The artwork in this book was rendered in graphite, watercolor and colored pencil, and completed digitally.

The text was set in Fournier.

Printed and bound in China

www.penguinrandomhouse.ca

1  2  3  4  5      23  22  21  20  19

Penguin
Random House
TUNDRA BOOKS

INSPIRED BY ANNE OF GREEN GABLES

# Anne's
## KINDRED SPIRITS

ADAPTED BY
## KALLIE GEORGE

PICTURES BY
## ABIGAIL HALPIN

tundra

# CHAPTER 1

The day dawned bright and cheery at Green Gables. Anne and Marilla were staring at three dresses on Anne's bed. They were all very plain. Anne wished they had puffed sleeves.

"Don't you like them?" asked Marilla.

"I can *imagine* I like them," said Anne.

Marilla sighed. "I don't want you to imagine. They're plain, sensible dresses. Now, put one on. We're going to see Mrs. Barry and her daughter Diana. Diana is your age."

"Oh!" Anne forgot about the puffed sleeves. More than puffed sleeves, Anne wished for a bosom friend, a kindred spirit who would be her best friend.

Now that she was living in Green Gables, most of her dreams had come true. Except that one.

"But, Marilla, what if Diana doesn't like me?" said Anne as they walked to Mrs. Barry's farm, Orchard Slope. "It would be the most *tragical* disappointment of my life."

"Don't get into a fluster. Just try not to make any of your strange speeches," said Marilla.

# CHAPTER 2

At Orchard Slope, Mrs. Barry opened the door.

"Is this the little girl you adopted?" she
asked Marilla.

Marilla nodded. "This is Anne."

"Anne with an *e*," said Anne.

"And how are you?" Mrs. Barry asked.

"I'm good in body, but rumpled in spirits,
ma'am," said Anne. Then, to Marilla, she said,
"That wasn't *too* strange, was it?"

Marilla raised her eyebrows.

Mrs. Barry did, too.

"Well, Anne, this is my little girl Diana.
Diana, why don't you take Anne out to play?"
said Mrs. Barry.

Diana was sitting on the couch, reading.
She looked up and gave Anne a merry smile.
Anne smiled back.

"Diana reads too much," Mrs. Barry added to Marilla, as Diana led Anne outside.

Diana loved reading, like Anne! And her hair was black as a raven's wing, not red. Anne did not like her own red hair. Anne thought Diana was perfect.

But would Diana like her?

# CHAPTER 3

Anne and Diana walked in the garden.
They looked at the flowers. Diana
picked some.

Anne was so nervous. She couldn't wait
any longer.

"Oh, Diana," said Anne. "Do you think you
could be my bosom friend?"

Diana laughed. Diana always laughed before she spoke. "I guess so," she said frankly. "It will be nice to have someone to play with."

"Will you *swear* to be my friend forever and ever?" asked Anne.

Diana looked shocked. "It's bad to swear!"

"Not this kind," said Anne quickly. "This kind is just promising solemnly."

"Well, I don't mind doing that," agreed Diana, relieved. "How do you do it?"

"You join hands — like so," said Anne. "And then you say: I solemnly swear to be faithful to my bosom friend as long as the sun and moon endure."

After, Diana laughed again. "You're a funny girl, Anne Shirley. But I think I will like you real well." She paused. "Next week there is going to be a Sunday school picnic with ice cream. Would you like to come?"

"Would I? Oh, Diana, I've never been to a picnic. I've dreamed of picnics, but . . ."

"So I suppose that's a yes?" giggled Diana.

"Oh, yes! Positively *yes*!"

# CHAPTER 4

The rest of the week Anne talked picnic and thought picnic and dreamed picnic.

"I can't wait," said Anne to Marilla when they were out driving in the carriage. "Although looking forward to things is half the pleasure of them."

"Really, Anne, can't you pay attention to anything other than the picnic?" said Marilla, fixing her amethyst brooch. It was very valuable.

"I don't know how *you* can pay attention when you have that on," said Anne. "I know I couldn't. It is *perfectly* elegant. Do you think amethysts might be the souls of flowers? You know, I've always wondered . . ."

Marilla sighed, as Anne kept going.

"At least she isn't talking about the picnic," Marilla thought.

# CHAPTER 5

The next day, Anne was shelling peas. Really, though, she was thinking about ice cream and what Diana might wear to the picnic. Diana had dresses with puffed sleeves.

Just then, Marilla came down from her room. Marilla was frowning.

"Anne, did you see my brooch? I thought I stuck it in my pincushion. But it isn't there."

Slowly Anne nodded.

"Did you touch it?" asked Marilla.

"Y-e-e-s," said Anne.

Marilla crossed her arms. "It isn't right to go into another person's room and touch things."

"I won't do it again," said Anne quickly. "That's one good thing about me. I never make the same mistake twice."

"Where did you put it?" asked Marilla.

"I put it back," said Anne.

Marilla went upstairs to check again. She returned a moment later. "Anne, the brooch is gone. You were the last person to touch it, by your own words. Now, tell me — did you lose it?"

"No," said Anne earnestly. "I did not. That's the truth! So there, Marilla."

Anne meant the "so there" to show how much she was telling the truth. But to Marilla it sounded rude.

"Go to your room at once, until you are ready to tell the truth!"

"Should I take the peas with me?" asked Anne meekly.

Marilla just pointed up to the east gable. "Go!"

# CHAPTER 6

Later, Marilla told Matthew, her brother, the story. Matthew was puzzled. But he had faith in Anne. Right from the start, he and Anne had been true kindred spirits.

"It didn't fall down behind your dresser?" he asked.

"I've looked everywhere," said Marilla. "Anne took it. That's the plain, ugly truth."

Marilla didn't know what to do.

That night, Marilla went up to Anne's room. Anne's eyes were red. Marilla felt a pang of pity. Still, she stood firm.

"You will stay up here until you confess, Anne."

"But the picnic is tomorrow," cried Anne. "You'll let me go to the picnic, won't you? I can't miss it, not when Diana is going to be there! I've never had a bosom friend before. Or been invited to a picnic. If you let me go, I will stay up here for as long as you want — *cheerfully*! But I *must* go to the picnic."

"You most certainly will not. Not until you confess."

Anne gasped. "Oh, Marilla!"

But Marilla had already shut the door.

# CHAPTER 7

The next day dawned, perfect for a picnic. Outside, Anne could just see Orchard Slope and Diana's window. Diana was probably getting ready for the picnic. She would wonder where Anne was.

There was only one thing Anne could do.

"I'm ready to confess," Anne said, when Marilla came in.

Marilla set down the breakfast tray. "Well, go on."

"You were right," said Anne. "I took the brooch. The temptation was *irresistible*. I pinned it on my breast. I imagined I was a fancy lady. It is so much easier to pretend you're a fancy lady when you are wearing a *real* amethyst brooch. I meant to put it back when you got home. As I was walking over the bridge, I took it off to look at it in the sunlight. Oh, how it shone! As I was leaning over . . . it slipped through my fingers . . . and went down, down, and sank forevermore beneath the Lake of Shining Waters."

She paused. "And that's the best I can do at confessing," she said.

Marilla's cheeks went hot.

"Anne, you . . . you are the wickedest girl!" she said.

"Yes, I am," replied Anne. "And I will need to be punished. But please do it quickly because I'd like to go to the picnic."

"Picnic! You will not go to the picnic. *That* is your punishment."

"No picnic!" exclaimed Anne. "But you said I could go if I confessed!"

"You are not going to the picnic. And that's final."

Anne flung herself on the bed and sobbed.

# CHAPTER 8

The day passed. Anne couldn't eat breakfast. Or lunch. Her heart was broken. How can you eat boiled greens when your heart is broken?

Marilla was upset, too. Matthew said she was being too hard on Anne. But he hadn't heard Anne's confession. "It seemed like she didn't even care that my brooch is lying at the bottom of the lake," said Marilla.

Marilla tried to keep herself busy. She washed the dishes. She made bread. Then she decided to mend her shawl. The shawl was in a box in her trunk.

As she took it out, she gasped. There, tangled in the shawl, was her brooch!

"Dear me!" cried Marilla. "Here's my brooch, safe and sound. I remember now when I took off my shawl, I laid it on top of my dresser. The brooch must have got caught in it!"

She went right up to Anne's room and showed it to her.

"Anne, why did you tell me you took it?" she asked.

"You said you'd keep me here until I confessed," replied Anne. "So I tried to make my confession as interesting as I could."

Marilla sighed. Her mouth twitched with a laugh. "You shouldn't have confessed to a thing you haven't done . . . but I should have believed you in the first place. If you forgive me, I'll forgive you. And then, you'd better get ready for the picnic."

Anne flew up in the air. "Oh, Marilla! Really?! There's still time?"

"It's only two o'clock," said Marilla. "You have plenty of time."

# CHAPTER 9

The picnic was perfect! Anne and Diana had
tea and rowed on the Lake of Shining Waters.
Jane Andrews nearly fell overboard! Anne
didn't even care that she was the only girl
with no puffed sleeves.

When Anne told Diana that she had almost
missed the picnic, she admitted, "I guess my
imagination can get me into trouble."

"I love your imagination, Anne," said Diana.

"We really are kindred spirits," sighed
Anne happily.

And when it came to the ice cream . . .

"Words fail me," Anne told Marilla that night.

"Well, that's a first," said Marilla. "But I am pleased you liked it. And that you and Diana get along so well."

When Anne went to bed, tired and happy, Marilla told Matthew, "I'm glad she got to go. She shouldn't have made up that story. Still, I should have believed her to begin with."

Marilla sighed. Then smiled.

"One thing's certain," she said at last. "No house will be dull as long as Anne Shirley lives in it."

And that was the truth.